This book belongs to

_____

™

THE LIMA BEAR STORIES

THE CAVE MONSTER

STORY BY

Thomas Weck *and* Peter Weck

ILLUSTRATIONS BY

Len DiSalvo

LIMA BEAR PRESS, LLC
Wilmington, Delaware

Published by Lima Bear Press, LLC

Lima Bear Press, LLC
2305 MacDonough Rd., Suite 201
Wilmington, DE 19805-2620
FOR VOLUME SALES: sales@limabearpress.com

Visit us on the web at
www.limabearpress.com

Printed in USA

Book & Cover design by: rosa+wesley, inc.

FIRST EDITION
ISBN: 978-1-933872-01-8

Weck, Thomas L., 1942-
    The cave monster / story by Thomas Weck and Peter Weck ; illustrations by Len DiSalvo. — 1st ed.

    p. : col. ill. ; cm. — (The Lima Bear stories)

    Summary: L. Joe Bean, Lima Bear's cousin, has been captured by the Cave Monster. Lima Bear and his friends enter the dangerous Black Cave to save L. Joe Bean. Will they save L. Joe Bean and themselves in time? The message of the story is: friends, individually afraid, find courage acting together.
    Interest age group: 004-008.
    ISBN: 978-1-933872-01-8

    1. Bears—Juvenile fiction. 2. Monsters—Juvenile fiction. 3. Caves—Juvenile fiction. 4. Friendship—Juvenile fiction. 5. Courage—Juvenile fiction. 6. Bears—Fiction. 7. Monsters—Fiction. 8. Caves—Fiction. 9. Friendship—Fiction. 10. Courage—Fiction. I. Weck, Peter (Peter M.) II. DiSalvo, Len. III. Title.

PZ7.W432 Cav 2011
[Fic]

CPSIA facility code: BP 312807

Lima Bear swung back and forth and waited for his cousin,
L. Joe Bean, to arrive. L. Joe Bean was a bear, and the same
tiny size as Lima Bear, although not green and furry. He was
smooth and dark red and looked like a pinto bean, instead of
a lima bean, like Lima Bear.

"Lima Bear! Lima Bear!" Whistle-Toe, the rabbit, dashed into view. "L. Joe Bean has been captured by the Cave Monster!"

"Oh, no! We must rescue him!" Lima Bear jumped off the swing.

Quickly, Lima Bear and Whistle-Toe gathered two other friends—Maskamal, the raccoon, and Back-Back, the opossum.

Back-Back was a very different kind of opossum. Looking at him from behind, he was invisible—as if he had disappeared, for, you see, he had no back.

"Where would the Cave Monster take him?" Whistle-Toe asked.

"To Black Cave," Lima Bear said.

"Bl-Bl-Black Cave?" Maskamal stammered. "I d-d-don't wanna go in there!"

Back-Back shivered and shook his head. "Me neither," he said.

Lima Bear pulled himself up to his very tallest and swallowed hard. "W- W- We have to," he said.

They discussed and argued about how best to save L. Joe Bean. Finally they decided it would be wisest to go at night in hopes that the Cave Monster would be asleep.

Lima Bear suggested that each of them go home and bring back something useful. They met again just before nightfall.

Whistle-Toe brought a canteen of water in case they got thirsty. Lima Bear brought two swords—his own, and L. Joe Bean's Royal Sword. It was special because it was gold with a diamond handle. Both little swords looked more like pins with tiny handles.

Maskamal brought a bow and arrow and a red flag. The bow was made of a large stick bent over and tied with a piece of string. The arrow was a smaller stick and had no point, so Maskamal had painted the tip red.

Back-Back could not think of anything useful to bring.

"That's all right," Maskamal said. "You can hold the red flag."

"What for?" Back-Back asked.

"I have a plan," Maskamal said. "When we see the Cave Monster, you wave this red flag at him, and when he goes after you I will shoot him with my bow and arrow. I'm a deadly shot. Here, I'll show you."

Back-Back stood next to a tree. He waved the red flag at the tree pretending it was the Cave Monster. Maskamal stood a few steps away, pulled the string of the bow as far back as he could and took aim.

The bow went 'Twa-a-a-ang'. The arrow fell out and landed next to Maskamal's foot.

"Um…," Lima Bear said, "you are going to have to be awfully close to the Cave Monster to hit him with that bow and arrow."

"Aw! This arrow's no good," Maskamal said and threw it away. "Let me try another one." He picked up a stick.

"But the tip isn't painted red," Lima Bear said.

"Oh, that's all right," Maskamal said.

He put it in his bow and aimed. 'Twa-a-a-ang'. The arrow flopped out of the bow and landed on his foot.

"There, you see," he said. "A straight shot. Just a little more distance, and it would have hit the tree dead center."

"I don't want to wave this flag at a real Cave Monster," Back-Back said.

"I know," Lima Bear said. "Let's tie my sword to the end of your arrow. That will give it a sharp point."

"Oh, yes!" Maskamal gave the stick to Lima Bear.

With some tiny thread, they tied Lima Bear's little needle-sword onto the end.

Maskamal was very happy with his new arrow with its sharp point. "Now that Cave Monster had better watch out!" he said.

The friends set out. Lima Bear was much too little to keep up, so he rode on Whistle-Toe's back. He held tight to the fur and watched the path ahead.

Soon they saw the dark entrance to Black Cave. They waited there, each expecting someone else to do something.

"Are you sure the Cave Monster is a-a-asleep?" Maskamal whispered.

"Of course he is," Whistle-Toe said, but he didn't sound very certain at all. "Still, we should be prepared, just in case he wakes up."

"O-o-okay," Maskamal said. "Back-Back, you stand near the cave and wave the flag. I'll stand over here with my bow and arrow." Maskamal moved far away from Black Cave—very far away.

"How are you going to hit him from there?" Back-Back called out. "Your arrow won't go that far."

"**Sh**hh! It will if I pull back on the string very hard. Besides, I-I-I can aim better from a distance."

The other three could see poor Maskamal's knees shaking from where they stood. And there they stood and waited…

and w a i t e d …

and w a i t e d …

and w a i t e d …

and w a i t e d …

and w a i t e d …

and w a i t e d …

and w a i t e d …

and w a i t e d .

"Hey Maskamal," Back-Back called out, "can I stop waving this flag? My arm is tired."

"I guess so. My arms are tired, too," Maskamal said.

Whistle-Toe looked at the sky. "It won't be dark much longer."

Lima Bear stood up tall, that is, tall for him. "I'll go in first," he declared.

That seemed to give them all courage. They marched into Black Cave. Lima Bear led the way, Back-Back was next, then Whistle-Toe followed by Maskamal, far behind and crouched low. Maskamal's paws were sweaty, and his whole body shook with fear.

Deeper into the cave they went. It was dark except for the flickering shadows from a fire. The Cave Monster had set a pot of water to boil and must have fallen asleep somewhere in the cave.

They all noticed L. Joe Bean tied up near the boiling pot. They knew that they needed to act quickly and quietly because any little noise could wake-up the sleeping Cave Monster.

"Oh, no. . . the Cave Monster is probably gonna make a soup out of L. Joe Bean!" Back-Back whispered.

"Not if I can help it!" Lima Bear declared quietly.

Lima Bear quickly tip-toed to L. Joe Bean and cut him loose with the Royal Sword and handed it to him.

Then, they heard a roar and saw the Cave Monster!

Back-Back frantically waved his flag!

Maskamal dropped his bow and arrow!

Whistle-Toe tried to hide behind his canteen!

L. Joe Bean thrust the Royal Sword into a fighting stance, and Lima Bear picked up a tiny pebble to throw!

The red flag did its job. The Cave Monster
headed for Back-Back. Back-Back was so afraid
that he laid down on his stomach to play dead
(that's what opossums do when they're in danger)
which of course made him disappear. Now the
Cave Monster saw nothing there so he turned
toward Maskamal.

Maskamal scrambled to pick up his bow and arrow just as the Cave Monster roared and started toward him. Whistle-Toe tried to stop the Cave Monster by throwing his canteen at him, but he missed.

L. Joe Bean and Lima Bear chased after the Cave Monster, but with their little legs they could not catch up.

Maskamal was so terrified that he shut his eyes tight, and pulled back on his bow with all his might. He pulled so hard that the bow pointed straight up.

'Twa-a-a-ang' The arrow flew up, up, up almost to the top of the cave, and then down, down, down and landed right on the Cave Monster's big toe. The Cave Monster howled with a terrible cry—a noise never heard before or since! And...

He jumped way up, up and down,

and tumbled and rumbled round and round.

He jumped so high, he jumped so fast

that into the side of the cave he crashed.

And the big, big rocks up on the wall

were shaken loose and they did fall.

They tumbled down and down and down

and buried the monster under the ground.

But the friends ran out, all safe and sound

and never again was the monster found.

The five friends raced out of the cave to safety just as the walls came crashing down!

"Maskamal, you were a great shot!" Lima Bear said. "And so brave," everyone agreed.

"Yes, I was, wasn't I." Maskamal said, feeling quite proud of himself.

L. Joe Bean was so thankful that he presented the Royal Sword to Maskamal. And Maskamal came to be known as the best archer of the forest.

THE END

EXTEND THE LEARNING

Read *The Cave Monster*

Before reading, you might:
- Ask children to close their eyes. Say the word 'monster' and then allow time for children to share what immediately comes to mind. *Close your eyes. What do you see when I say the word 'monster'?*
- Build background knowledge by sharing information about caves. Let children know a cave is a large hole. Caves can be found underground or in the side of a mountain. Very little light is seen in a cave. You often find animals living in caves, such as bats, bears, and foxes.
- Read the title and briefly discuss the cover illustration. *What do you think might happen in this story?*
- *Let's read* The Cave Monster *to find out how Lima Bear and his friends work together to outsmart the Cave Monster.*

During reading, stop and ask children questions to make sure they are following along. Take time to talk about details in the illustrations to help children understand story concepts and unfamiliar vocabulary. Ask questions such as:
- (page 3) *How does the author let you know the characters are afraid of the Cave Monster?*

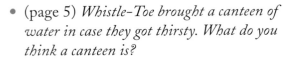
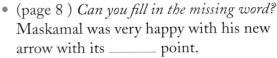

- (page 5) *Whistle-Toe brought a canteen of water in case they got thirsty. What do you think a canteen is?*
- (page 8) *Can you fill in the missing word?* Maskamal was very happy with his new arrow with its _____ point.
- (page 15) *Maskamal's paws were sweaty, and his whole body shook with fear. What do you think sweaty means? Tell me how your hands get sweaty?*
- (page 19) *How does the illustration help you understand that the Cave Monster is gigantic?*
- (page 23) *What happened after the arrow landed on the Cave Monster's big toe?*

After reading, take time to talk about the book. You might ask:
- *Tell me what this story was about.*
- *What parts of the story did you find interesting?*
- *Let's look for details in the story that tell us about L. Joe Bean and Lima Bear. How were L. Joe Bean and Lima Bear alike? How were they different?*
- *Lima Bear told his friends to go home and find something useful to help rescue L. Joe Bean. Can you recall what each character brought? What would you bring?*
  Maskamal (bow and arrow)
  Whistle-Toe (canteen)
  Lima Bear (2 tiny swords)
- *How would it feel to walk into a deep, dark cave?*
- *Would you be afraid of the Cave Monster? Why or why not?*
- *Tell me why you think the author wrote the last part of the story as a rhyme.*

ACTIVITIES

- **Make a Monster Poster.**   Use colorful markers to create a Cave Monster poster. Ask children questions, such as *What does the Cave Monster look like? What did the Cave Monster do? Where does the Cave Monster live?* Have children think of descriptive words to include in a simple description about the Cave Monster. Have them think of details that tell how the monster looks, feels, or sounds. Don't forget to add a colorful picture to go along with the description.

- **Words with Multiple Meanings.**   Maskamal brought a bow and arrow to help rescue L. Joe Bean. Draw attention to the word *bow*. Ask what bow means in this context (a curved piece of wood with a string attached to it for shooting arrows). Talk about how the word *bow* has another meaning: A bow is also something made out of string or ribbon that has two loops. Remind children how good readers need to figure out what a word means in the context of the story. Look for other words in the story that have multiple meanings such as *swing* (page 2), *tie*, (page 8), and *wave* (page 13).

- **Sponge Ball Target Practice.**   Maskamal pulls the string of the bow and takes aim at a tree. That's his target. Make a sponge ball for target practice. Use three brand new $1/2 \times 2\,3/4 \times 4\,1/4$-inch sponges. Use scissors to cut six $1/2$-inch strips. Repeat with the other two sponges. Place the strips on top of each other. Cinch the strips across the middle with a piece of string and make a tight knot. Scatter targets on tree trunks or fence posts. Then take turns tossing the sponges at each of the targets. Count how many tosses it takes to hit the center of the targets.

- **Word Sort.**   Draw attention to different ways the long *e* sound is spelled in words: *e, ee,* and *ea*. Work with children to highlight the following words in the story.
    e: he, be
    ee: sleep, keep, see, three, knee, deeper
    ea: each, bean
List the words on a piece of paper. Slowly say each word aloud. Tell children to listen to the sound the vowel pattern makes in each word. Ask volunteers to use a highlighter to mark the long *e* spelling in each word.

each

bean

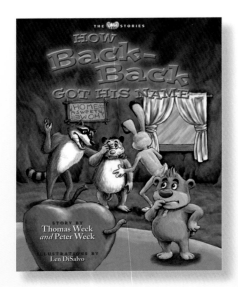

Can you imagine what it would be like to lose your back!!? Well, that is exactly what happens to Plumpton, the Opossum. Lima Bear and his clever friends become detectives searching for his missing back. Follow them as they try new and different ways of thinking to solve the mystery. See how they band together to protect each other in times of danger! Will they ever find Plumpton's back? Follow the story to find the answer.

THE MESSAGE OF THE STORY IS:
The tolerance of differences in others yields benefits.

$15.95

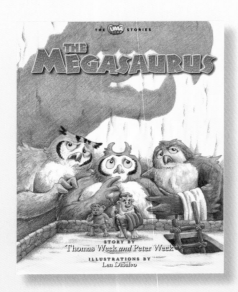

What's the King of Beandom to do? The tiny, multi-colored bean-shaped bears of Beandom are under attack by a monster. Even the King's wisest advisors seem unable to find a solution. Who will save Beandom? Can an ordinary tiny bear step forward with a plan that works?

Welcome to Beandom! It's a great place to visit. Or, it will be—just as soon as we get rid of that pesky monster!

THE MESSAGE OF THE STORY IS:
Follow your convictions even when others think differently.

$15.95

FORTHCOMING BOOKS BY LIMA BEAR PRESS, LLC

The Labyrinth

The Search for Back-Back's Back

Lima Bear's Halloween

★ IT'S MY STATE! ★

Mississippi

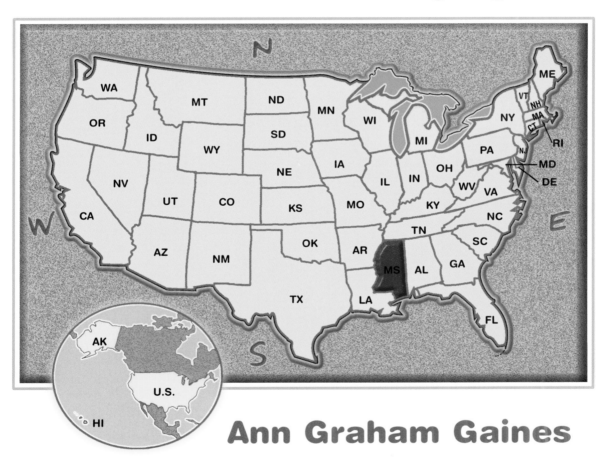

Ann Graham Gaines

Marshall Cavendish
Benchmark
New York

Marshall Cavendish Benchmark
99 White Plains Road
Tarrytown, New York 10591-9001
www.marshallcavendish.us

Library of Congress Cataloging-in-Publication Data

Gaines, Ann.
Mississippi / by Ann Graham Gaines.
p. cm. — (It's my state!)
Includes bibliographical references and index.
ISBN-13: 978-0-7614-2214-3
ISBN-10: 0-7614-2214-5
1. Mississippi—Juvenile literature. I. Title.
F341.3.G35 2007
976.2—dc22
2006034090

Photo research by Candlepants, Inc.

Cover Photo: Corbis

Back cover illustration: The license plate shows Mississippi's state flower, the magnolia.

The photographs in this book are used by permission and through the courtesy of: *Corbis:* Pete Saloutos, 4 (top); Michael T. Sedam, 4 (lower); D. Robert & Lorri Franz, 4 (center); Stuart Westmorland, 5 (top); Roy Morsch, 5 (lower); Buddy Mays, 11, 67; Raymond Gehman, 13; Joe McDonald, 19 (top); Dave Bartruff, 19 (center); Bettmann, 20, 37 (lower), 51 (lower), 60; Danny Lehman, 23; PoodlesRock, 26; Nik Wheeler, 27, 49; 32, 34, 37 (top), 50 (top), 50 (center); Flip Schulke, 36, 57; Dennis Marisco, 43; Philip Gould, 45, 46, 47, 72 (top); 73 (top); Dan Guravich, 48; William Coupon, 50 (lower); Reuters, 51 (top), 69; John Springer Collection, 51 (center); Owaki-Kulla, 62; Jim Richardson, 63; Dave G. Houser/Post-Housertock, 68; Richard Hamilton Smith, 72 (lower); Scott Stulberg, 72 (center). *Photo Researchers Inc.:* Richard Ellis, 5 (center); Kenneth Murray, 73 (center). *Clint Farlinger:* 9, 18 (center). *The Image Works:* Photri/Topham, 12; Joseph Sohm, 38; Jeff Greenberg, 73 (lower). *Alex Demyan:* 15 (both). *Michael Durham:* 18 (top). *Copyright Michael Forsberg / www.michaelforsberg.com:* 18 (lower). *Tom & Pat Leeson:* 19 (lower). *Mississippi Development Authority/Division of Tourism:* 41, 52. *Super Stock:* age fotostock, 53, 54. *Envision:* Rita Maas, 66.

Series design by Anahid Hamparian
Printed in Malaysia

1 3 5 6 4 2

Contents

A Quick Look at Mississippi   4

⭐1 The Magnolia State   7
Plants & Animals   18

⭐2 From the Beginning   21
Making a Shell Gorget   25
Important Dates   37

⭐3 The People   39
Famous Mississippians   50
Calendar of Events   52

⭐4 How It Works   55
Branches of Government   58

⭐5 Making a Living   63
Recipe for Sweet and Spicy Pecans   66
Products & Resources   72

State Flag and Seal   75
State Map   76
State Song   77
More About Mississippi   78
Index   79

A Quick Look at Mississippi

Nickname: Magnolia State
Population: 2,921,088 (2005 estimate)
Statehood: December 10, 1817

Flower and Tree: Magnolia

In 1900, more than half of Mississippi's schoolchildren voted for the magnolia blossom as their favorite flower. Students voted again in the early 1930s for their favorite tree. Once more, the magnolia came out on top. Wild magnolia trees can grow to be 60 feet or more. Their heavily scented flowers, which blossom in the spring, come in white and cream.

Bird: Mockingbird

The gray and white mockingbird, which is seen all over Mississippi, is a loud and energetic singer. The bird mimics other birds' songs, and that is why "mocking" is part of its name.

Land Mammal: White-Tailed Deer

The white-tailed deer was named Mississippi's official state land mammal in 1974. Found in woods all over the state, male deer, or stags, grow large racks of antlers. The females, known as does, are smaller. Fawns, or very young deer, have spotted fur when they are born. This helps them hide.

Water Mammal: Bottlenose Dolphin

Not every state has an official water mammal, but Mississippi does. The bottlenose dolphin, also called a porpoise, lives off the coast of Mississippi in the deep waters of the Gulf of Mexico. A member of the whale family, the bottlenose has sharp teeth, a small snout, and a dorsal fin on its back. It breathes through a blowhole located on top of its head. Dolphins are sociable creatures and live and travel in pods, or groups.

Fossil: Prehistoric Whale

Fifty million years ago, Mississippi was covered by an ocean that was filled with life. One of the most amazing creatures to swim those waters was the prehistoric whale, also known as the zeuglodon. This creature could grow to be 80 feet long. It had vertebrae (individual bones in its spine) that were more than 1 foot long. In 1981, the Mississippi state government declared the prehistoric whale as the official state fossil.

Fish: Largemouth Bass

A fisherman's favorite, largemouth bass flourish in Mississippi's lakes and rivers. Most largemouth bass, named for their wide mouths, have greenish to blackish backs and pale bellies. The largest known to have been caught in Mississippi weighed in at more than 18 pounds. The largemouth bass has been the state's official fish since 1974.

The Magnolia State

Country singer and world traveler, Charlie Pride, has said of his home state: "I loved Mississippi and do to this day. The rainbows that stretch from horizon to horizon after a summer rain are the most spectacular I have ever seen." For a small state—just thirty-second in size compared with other states—Mississippi's landscapes are spectacular. The state runs about 350 miles from north to south and 140 miles from east to west. Within those 47,716 square miles are rolling hills, slow-moving waterways called bayous, rushing streams, large and small rivers, farmland, sleepy towns, and several bustling cities.

Mississippi's Location

Situated on the Gulf of Mexico, Mississippi is a part of the United States that geographers call the Deep South. In terms of both geography

Mississippi's Borders

North: Tennessee
South: Louisiana and the Gulf of Mexico
East: Alabama
West: The Mississippi River, Louisiana, and Arkansas

and way of life, the state is often grouped with Louisiana, which sits to the west, and Alabama and Georgia, to the east.

Mississippi's shape is almost a rectangle, but not quite. The Mississippi River forms the state's western boundary. As the river weaves in and out, so does the state's western border. Louisiana cuts a small notch into Mississippi's rectangular shape.

A Rich Land

Three important physical features shaped Mississippi's landscape. The southern end of the Appalachian Mountains, a long mountain chain that runs all along the United States' eastern seaboard, turns into hills in Mississippi. One peak, Woodall Mountain, rises 806 feet above sea level, Mississippi's highest point.

An even greater influence than the Appalachians on Mississippi's land is its major river. The Mississippi River begins as a narrow stream, just 20 to 30 feet wide, up north in Minnesota. By the time its waters reach the state of Mississippi, over 400 miles later, the river is 2 miles wide in some parts. For thousands of years, the river's ever-changing waters have built up a broad flat delta in the western part of Mississippi. Also called an alluvial plain, the delta is an area where the river's floodwaters have deposited a thick layer of rich, black soil over the land.

The Mississippi River has also created special water features called oxbow lakes. Many of these lakes formed naturally over a long period of time. The loops became cut off from the rest of the river and formed small, curved lakes. Others have formed when engineers reshaped the river with dams to control flooding. These engineering projects isolated loops of water that became oxbow lakes.

Rain that falls on these Mississippi River headwaters in Minnesota takes ninety days to reach Mississippi.

To the south of the state lies the Gulf of Mexico. Measured in a straight line, Mississippi's coastline is 40 miles long. However, its coastline is anything but straight. Many bays and coves cut into the land along the southern coastline. If you followed all the ins and outs of these inlets, you would discover that the shoreline actually measures around 350 miles. Pounded by waves in many places, the shape of the coastline shifts constantly. A chain of small islands along the shore offers some protection for the mainland from storms that the Gulf blows in.

Millions of years ago, at many different times, ocean waters covered the land that is now the state of Mississippi. When the sea creatures and plants that lived in these seas died, they decayed, and their remains drifted to the ocean floor. They became oil and gas deposits, which are valuable Mississippi resources today.

Mississippi's Waters

Abundant waterways make Mississippi a very green state. Rivers of all sizes flow across the land. While the Mississippi River is the state's largest river, it is just one of many. The state also has numerous bayous. These marshy streams move so slowly, they hardly seem to move at all. Some bayous connect lakes and rivers in what is called the Delta Region of the state. Other bayous to the south empty into inland waters, then into the Gulf of Mexico.

Through the western part of the state flow tributaries—other rivers whose waters eventually empty into the Mississippi River. These tributaries include the Yalobusha and Tallahatchie rivers, which meet just north of the city of Greenwood, and form a single river, called the Yazoo. This important waterway runs south and west until it reaches the city of Vicksburg and the Mississippi River. Running a similar course, the Big Black River crosses the state from east to west before emptying into the Mississippi River.

The central and eastern parts of the state are covered by smaller rivers and creeks that grow in size as they run south toward the Gulf of Mexico. These include the Pascagoula and the Chickasawhay rivers as well as the much larger Pearl River.

The Tennessee-Tombigbee Waterway—or Tenn-Tom—is a man-made canal completed in 1984. It joins the Tombigbee and Tennessee Rivers.

In the northeastern part of the state, the Tombigbee River runs south into Alabama, where it continues its course to the Gulf of Mexico.

Mississippi has many lakes, the largest of which are reservoirs that have been created by damming rivers. Among such bodies of water are the Ross Barnett Reservoir on the Pearl River;

Paddle wheelers, steamboats, barges, and freighters replaced the dugout canoes that Native Americans once rowed along the Mississippi River.

Arkabutla Lake on the Coldwater River; Grenada Lake on the Yalobusha River; and the Pickwick Lake on the Tennessee River.

The Delta Region

Some geographers divide the state into two regions: the Alluvial Plain, or Delta, to the west, and the East Gulf Coastal Plain. But Mississippians usually think of their state as having five distinct regions: the Delta Region, the River Capital Region, the Hills Region, the Pines Region, and the Coastal Region.

The Delta Region is located between the Mississippi and the Yazoo rivers. This flat area frequently floods, spreading silt, a kind of soil, along the way. Rich soil, in an area called bottomlands, supports huge trees, luscious plants and vines, as well as many of Mississippi's agricultural crops. Outcroppings, called bluffs, rise from the riverbanks in parts of the Delta Region where the Mississippi River has cut a path over time.

The River or Capital Region

Mississippians tend to refer to the southwestern corner of their state as the River or Capital Region. The area, bound by the Mississippi River on the west and the Pearl River on the east, stretches south to the dividing line between Mississippi and Louisiana. The cities of Vicksburg and Jackson are on the northern border of the area. The Capital Region looks like the

Satellite images of the Mississippi River like this one taken in 2001, track the constant changes the river makes in the delta.

Delta Region, with river bluffs, flat land, and many bayous and oxbow lakes. But unlike the Delta Region, Mississippi's Capital Region is more heavily populated.

One population center is Jackson. It is not only the state's capital but also Mississippi's largest city. Suburbs and small towns have grown up around Jackson. Parts of the region look like places all across the United States, with housing developments, strip malls, and parking lots. Not all of the construction in this area is modern, however. In some parts of Jackson, historical Southern architecture has been preserved.

Mississippi is one of most rural states in the nation. In 1990, only about 47 percent of all Mississippians lived in areas defined as urban. More than half the population lives in rural areas.

The Hills Region

In the northeastern part of the state is a hilly section called the Hills Region. In the extreme northeastern corner of the Hills Region are the sandy Tennessee River Hills. To the west, in the center of this area, is Pontotoc Ridge. The Appalachian Mountains begin their rise in the north, into Tennessee. Much of this part of the Hills Region is wooded. The federal government established two national forests here. Three more towns in this region are Corinth, Oxford, and Tupelo, the birthplace of Elvis Presley.

The Pines

Early explorers describe the area that is now Mississippi as a forested land. Today a broad band of piney woods cuts across the center of the state, which Mississippians call the Pines Region. This area stretches from the Hills Region up to the coastal plain. Lumbering and farming centers lie in cleared areas of these forests. Like the Delta to its west and the Hills to its north, this region is sparsely populated.

The Natchez Trace Parkway follows the same route as a historic American trail through forests and swamps.

The Coastal Region

To the south of the Pines Region is the Coastal Region along the Gulf of Mexico. A string of islands lies offshore in the Gulf of Mexico. In 1969, Hurricane Camille split Ship Island in two. One half of the former island is now called East Ship Island. It is a place where ships have anchored ever since the British Navy stayed there during the War of 1812.

The part of the Gulf that lies between these coastal islands and the rest of the state is called the Mississippi Sound, a long and shallow body of water. There are large bays at the towns of Bay St. Louis and Pascagoula. As the Pearl and Pascagoula rivers flow into the sound, they form wide deltas with marshes and swampland.

In this region are the old port cities of Biloxi, Gulfport, Pascagoula, and Bienville. Visitors flock to the white beaches along Mississippi's shoreline with its many resorts and campgrounds. Just up from the coast, a series of sand steps or terraces have formed from sand that blows in from the Gulf.

The Gulf Intracoastal Waterway, a 1,100-mile-long system of rivers, canals, and bays, stretches from northwest Florida to Brownsville, Texas. The Mississippi Sound, a bay that separates the state's islands from the coast, forms the Gulf Intracoastal Waterway's midsection.

Climate

Mississippi's rivers, lakes, bayous, ocean, and warm climate make it a hot, humid place for much of the year. Temperatures seldom dip below 50 degrees Fahrenheit in the winter but can reach the eighties and nineties in the summer. The heavy, wet heat contributes to the slow pace of life in the state.

But life is not always sleepy or slow in Mississippi. Hurricanes regularly threaten the state, especially along its Gulf Coast.

Hurricane Camille hit Mississippi hard in 1969. But even people who survived Camille agree that Hurricane Katrina hit harder when it roared into Mississippi on August 29, 2005. Winds measured 145 miles per hour when Katrina made landfall in Louisiana. That made it the third-strongest hurricane ever to hit the United States. Then the hurricane skipped along the shore a little farther east. It came ashore for a second time, this time at the Louisiana/Mississippi border. The winds had decreased a little, but they still measured 125 miles per hour. Not only did the wind cause great damage, so did a huge storm surge. This powerful moving wall of water rushed into Mississippi's coastal cities. Most of the buildings along the shore were wiped out or heavily damaged. One storm surge in Biloxi—measured at 30 feet—was the largest ever recorded in the United States. Katrina's winds and storm surges also caused great damage to Waveland, Bay St. Louis, Pass Christian, Long Beach, Gulfport, Ocean Springs, Gautier, and Pascagoula.

In addition to the devastating hurricane, eleven tornadoes accompanied Katrina in Mississippi. Two of them were rated as F2s. That means the tornadoes packed winds of anywhere between 113 to 157 miles per hour.

Oceanfront houses in Bay St. Louis, which had survived previous hurricanes, were no match for Hurricane Katrina in 2005.

As of December 7, 2005, officials determined that 235 Mississippians died during the hurricane, 68 people were still missing, and 68,700 homes and businesses were destroyed. Affected families had to find temporary places to live in shelters, trailers, and in the homes of relatives or even strangers who lived in safer areas. When President George W. Bush toured the state in May of 2006, he expressed admiration for the people of the state who were working hard to rebuild. He said that Mississippians showed "a strength that wind and water can never take away."

Today, the people of Mississippi continue to redevelop areas that Katrina destroyed. Experts in climate and water control, along with architects, are advising Mississippians on how to rebuild. Some new development will be pushed farther back from waterfront areas. This will create buffer zones of land that can help absorb the flooding that accompanies hurricanes. New buildings will be designed high enough and strong enough to withstand powerful winds and rising water. A new coastal Mississippi is on the way!

Mississippi's Wild Places

In a state where over half the land is covered with forest, there is something for every nature lover. The forested areas are filled with a wide variety of trees, wildlife, and wildflowers.

The northern forests of Mississippi support hardwoods, including elm, hickory, and oak, as well as evergreens. The town of Tupelo is named after a special gum tree that flourishes in swamps and other wet places. Several kinds of pine trees—the longleaf, slash pine, and loblolly—grow mainly in the south.

White-tailed deer live everywhere in the state, often moving out from the forests into populated areas. Mississippi's forests and fields are also home to wild hogs, black bears, squirrels, foxes, opossums, rabbits, raccoons, and skunks.

Mississippi's forests shelter a variety of birds, such as the eastern wild turkey, bobwhite quail, mourning dove, and the woodcock. Birdwatchers thrill at the sight of the red-cockaded woodpecker, a bird that is on the rare and endangered species list.

Mississippi's wildflowers and tree blossoms burst into color in the spring. These include pink and red wild azaleas, creamy magnolias, black-eyed Susans, pale pink camellias, purple and white iris, pink and white dogwood blossoms, violets, tiny trillium flowers in whites, yellows, and reds, and the ivory Cherokee rose, which Native Americans first cultivated in the area.

Mississippi's wild wetlands also shelter large numbers of animals and birds. Millions of water birds such as ducks, geese, and swans live in rivers, streams, and bayous. Egrets, herons, and terns nest along the coastal shorelines and the banks of Mississippi's rivers and lakes. Alligators, snapping turtles, and water snakes, including the venomous, or poisonous, cottonmouth, populate the state's waterways. Bass, bream, catfish, croaker, and perch swim in Mississippi's fresh waters. Other creatures found in coastal waters include saltwater fish, such as mackerel, menhaden, big tarpon, as well as shellfish such as crabs, oysters, and shrimp.

The state of Mississippi protects a number of its endangered animals. Black bears, Florida panthers, gray bats, Indiana bats, all sea turtles, gopher tortoises, sawback turtles (black-knobbed, ringed, yellow-blotched), black pine snakes, eastern indigo snakes, rainbow snakes, and southern hognose snakes, are on the endangered animals list in Mississippi.

Plants & Animals

Pitcher Plant

Pitcher plants grow in the damp bogs of Mississippi. They resemble pitchers because they hold water. These plants also devour insects. The plant's sweet nectar attracts insects into its tube-shaped leaves. Once inside, the insects become trapped in the hairs that cover the leaf's interior. Enzymes, which are juices at the bottom of the leafy tube, break down the insects so that the plant can digest them and use them as food.

Bald Cypress

Long ago, ancient forests of bald cypresses grew in swamp water or near the Mississippi River. Bald cypresses can still be seen in Mississippi, but many of these majestic trees have been cut down for their valuable timber. The tall, old trees have knobby roots and branches of needles, rather than leaves.

Sandhill Crane

Mississippi's sandhill cranes are an endangered species. Standing about 4 feet tall, with a nearly 6-foot wingspan, they have long legs and necks. Their feathers are shades of gray. Sandhill cranes have a red crown, white cheek patches, and black legs. The call of a sandhill crane is a loud, distinctive, croaking sound.

American Alligator

For a time, American alligators were an endangered species. But today their numbers are growing. In 2001, biologists estimated that approximately 32,000 to 38,000 alligators lived in Mississippi's many waterways. Male alligators grow up to 15 feet long. The average gator has seventy-five teeth.

Oyster

Oysters are a type of mollusk with a rough shell that is irregular in shape, rather than rounded and smooth like a clam. They live in coastal waters, attached to rocks on the ocean floor. Oysters are filter feeders that eat plankton, the tiny plants and animals that float in water. Oysters are so well adapted to the waters off the coast of Mississippi that they are now grown there to be sold as food.

Black Bear

Mississippi's hardwood bottomlands once supported large populations of black bear. These small bears—4 to 7 feet in length and weighing less than 500 pounds—nearly died out in the twentieth century. Excessive hunting, and the disappearance of hardwood forests due to lumbering and farming, decreased the black bear population. In 1984, wildlife experts listed the black bear as endangered. They currently estimate that there are fewer than fifty bears in the entire state.

From the Beginning

Thousands of years ago, humans came to live on the land that would one day become Mississippi. The land was an ideal place for these hunting and gathering people to settle down. Its many rivers provided water to drink, fish to eat, and an easy way to travel and trade goods. The forests were full of animals to hunt for food and wood to use for building simple shelters and dugout canoes. These early people soon discovered that they did not always have to hunt animals and gather fruit and nuts for all their food. They could settle down and grow some of the food they needed in the area's rich soil.

The Mississippi River gave these early groups so much that many of them considered it to be the center of the universe. Archaeologists, the scientists who study the past, have found evidence that these early people built small cities and farming communities in several areas of the land that is now Mississippi. The archaeologists have unearthed stone and metal tools, weapons, pottery, masks, and engraved seashells that indicate busy, successful communities. These experts believe that the

Some families left Mississippi to look for work during the Great Depression of the 1930s.

ancient people they call Mound Builders built the huge mounds of earth located around Mississippi and other nearby states. These early people probably honored their leaders and their dead by building the chiefs' homes and temples on the flat tops of some of these mounds. Since other mounds had protective stockades around them, the Mound Builders likely used forts to defend their land, their crops, their riches, and their communities.

The Native Groups

Experts believe that over time the descendents of the Mound Builders organized themselves into separate villages and groups. These communities survived by hunting, fishing, and farming. The people used dugout canoes to travel and trade along the coastal shores and on the rivers. They probably lived in shelters made of leaves and wooden poles or log houses plastered with clay from nearby riverbanks. Living in separate areas, these individual communities eventually developed their own languages and customs.

One such group was the Chickasaw, a proud and fierce people. Some experts believe the Chickasaw and the Choctaw may have been part of one group in earlier times. Spread across Mississippi, Alabama, Tennessee, and Kentucky, the Chickasaw were semi-nomadic. They moved part-time and settled along waterways within their territory at other times. Members of their group hunted, gathered, and grew enough food to feed their own people. Chickasaw society was well organized, with strong leaders and good lines of communication. Runners carried messages along the Chickasaw network to far-scattered people whenever they needed to hold a meeting, or council.

Today's Chickasaw remain a proud people, who describe themselves as "unconquered and unconquerable."

The Natchez people used natural grasses and clay to build dwellings similar to this one shown at Grand Village, a reconstructed community in Natchez, Mississippi.

Chickasaw defenses were so strong that they boasted their members were almost never captured or killed.

To the south and east into Alabama lived the Choctaw, a forest people who also farmed and traded. Like the other groups in the area, the Choctaw were well organized. Their central government included courts where elders could listen to group members' complaints and settle them.

Many Choctaw males had sloping flat foreheads. Ethnologists (the historians who study ancient people) believed members of the group pressed boards against boy babies' foreheads to

Choctaw soldiers serving in the United States Army in World War I used a code to pass along important military information. It was based on their language so the enemy could not understand the code.

give them their distinctive shape. This made them identifiable as Choctaw and set them apart from the men of other Native groups. Early European noted that the Choctaw were fast runners who also loved to play ball games. Players sometimes peacefully settled disputes with other native groups by playing stickball.

The Natchez people lived along the Mississippi River. At least five hundred years ago, they used the river's waters and rich bottomlands to grow corn, squash, and beans. They organized their society into separate classes of nobility (rulers) and commoners (ordinary people). The Natchez had one supreme ruler, called the Great Sun, who was so honored that he was carried everywhere so he never had to touch the ground.

Many of the place names in Mississippi come from Native American languages, such as Biloxi, Yazoo, and Pascagoula. According to Muriel H. Wright, a historian who wrote a book about the history of the Mississippi River, the Chippewa word "Mississippi" has been translated as "great river" or "gathering of waters." According to Choctaw legend, when their ancestors came upon the river, they exclaimed, "Misha sipokni!" That has been translated as "Here is a river that is beyond all age!"

Making a Shell Gorget

Shell gorgets (pronounced *gorjets*) were carved-shell ornaments found in some Mississippi Valley burial sites, dating from about 1000 to 1600 CE. Images on the gorgets included rattlesnakes, falcons, a "birdman" with human and bird features, and many other natural images. Follow these instructions to make your own gorgets.

What You Need

large clean shells of any kind (you can
collect them from outside or buy
    some at crafts supply shops)
pencil
thin-point markers
3-foot lengths of cord or ribbon
strong glue

Designing a shell gorget:

Decide on an animal, bird, reptile, or other image from nature for your shell gorget. In pencil, sketch your design inside the shell.

Once you are happy with the design, trace over your pencil markings with a marker.

Tie the ends of the cord or ribbon into a small tight knot. Rest this knot on the back of your shell. Use the strong glue to make the ribbon stick to the shell. When the glue is dry you might also want to use strong tape to make sure the shell sticks to the ribbon.

Wear the gorget, give it as a gift, or hang it to display it to your friends and family!

This painting by William Powell portrays Spanish explorer Hernando De Soto's discovery of the Mississippi River in 1541. Historians believe De Soto died on the banks of the river one year later.

Natives and Europeans Meet

The Spanish explorer Hernando De Soto and an army of several hundred soldiers became the first Europeans ever to see what is now the state of Mississippi. Searching for treasure in 1540, the members of this expedition began their explorations in Florida and ended beyond the Rio Grande River in the Southwest. When De Soto's group passed through the area that is present-day Mississippi, it encountered members of three Native American nations: the Natchez, the Choctaw, and the Chickasaw. The Chickasaw were the people with whom De Soto had the most contact. But the group did not welcome the contact. They attacked De Soto's party several times until the Spaniards left the area.

In 1673, 130 years after De Soto's visit to America, the French explorers Jacques Marquette and Louis Jolliet came down the Mississippi River. They turned around when they reached a village at the mouth of the Arkansas River, populated by Native Americans called the Arkansas. The two explorers did not travel any farther because they feared meeting enemy Spaniards, who were also exploring the area.

In 1682, René-Robert Cavelier Sieur de LaSalle, another French explorer, also traveled down the Mississippi River to the Gulf of Mexico. LaSalle recorded meeting people of the Taensa, Natchez, and Choctaw groups. When LaSalle reached the mouth of the Mississippi, he claimed all the land along the huge river on behalf of his ruler, King Louis XIV of France.

In the years that followed, the French made several efforts to create colonies on the land LaSalle had claimed. They wanted to prevent their Spanish rivals to the south from gaining complete control of the land that would eventually become the southern part of the United States. In 1699, Pierre LeMoyne d'Iberville brought two hundred settlers to a location in what is the present-day Bay of Biloxi. The group built Fort Maurepas. According to d'Iberville's plans, this would become the first capital of French Louisiana.

This historical reenactment photo shows the French commander Pierre LeMoyne d'Iberville and his party landing in 1699 on the shores the Gulf of Mexico, which they claimed for France.

Eventually the French built several plantations around Fort Maurepas. In 1719, the plantation owners imported slaves from Africa and forced these slaves to work without pay in the cotton, tobacco, rice, and indigo fields.

In the meantime, the British had also started colonies in North America. That led to conflicts with the French. Soon the British and French engaged in what would be called the French and Indian War, which lasted from 1754 to 1763. (The French and Indian War refers to fighting that occurred between the French, who were supported by their Native American allies, and the British, who had their own Native American allies in the fight.) After the British defeated the French, Great Britain gained all of France's territories east of the Mississippi River, with the exception of the city of New Orleans. British government officials in London made southern Mississippi part of the British colony of West Florida. Northern Mississippi became part of Britain's Georgia colony.

Meanwhile trouble was brewing in the British colonies. In 1775, many colonists became frustrated with the British rulers and began the American Revolution. However, the people who lived in what is now Mississippi did not become involved in the fighting of that war. Most residents of West Florida were Loyalists, or Tories, who remained loyal to Britain's King George III. They hoped the British redcoats would win the war. But in 1781, the war directly affected the people of West Florida. Spain took control of West Florida while the British were fighting the French. When the Revolution came to an end two years later, the colonies separated from Great Britain and became the United States. Great Britain formally recognized Spain as West Florida's owner. Spain granted some northern land to the newly formed United States.

In 1795, a new treaty stated that West Florida's northern boundary was changed. This meant that most of present-day Mississippi became part of the United States.

The Mississippi Territory

In 1798, the federal government organized this newly acquired land into the Mississippi Territory. Roughly twice the size of the state today, this territory reached from the Chattahoochee River on the east to the Mississippi River on the west. The territory included most of the present-day states of Alabama and Mississippi.

In 1803, the United States expanded when President Thomas Jefferson completed the Louisiana Purchase. That added close to 3 million square miles of western land to the United States, including the city of New Orleans. Americans became more involved in trade up and down the Mississippi River. One year later, the United States government extended the territory's boundary farther north than it had been. The territory included everything up to the southern border of Tennessee.

In 1810, British settlers in West Florida threw off Spanish rule and declared themselves the independent Republic of West Florida. However, President James Madison had other ideas. He made the republic part of the United States. Two years later, West Florida was formally attached to the eastern part of the territory of Mississippi.

Statehood

By 1817, the population of the Mississippi Territory had grown so much, the federal government divided it in two. The western half was admitted into the Union as the state of Mississippi.

The eastern half became the Alabama Territory, which became a state in 1819.

Plantation owners continued to buy more slaves to do the backbreaking work of growing cotton in ever-larger fields. Cotton made

Mississippi's Native Americans struggled long and hard in their attempts to keep their land. But by 1832, the various groups had signed over almost all of it to the United States and moved onto reservations in other states. One group that did not leave the state was the Choctaw.

Mississippi one of the richest states in the Union. Several wealthy white families lived in huge plantation homes or in elegant mansions in the busy, cultured city of Natchez. However, Mississippi had many more white families who farmed small pieces of land or ran small businesses. Mississippi's large black population included a few hundred free blacks who lived and worked in the state. The slave

Profits from slave labor helped build elegant plantations, such as Stanton Hall in Natchez, Mississippi. Many plantations can be visited today.

population, however, numbered in the tens of thousands. Natchez had the second largest slave market in the United States, where about 200,000 slaves were bought and sold.

The lives of slaves were largely ones of endless work. Owners sometimes split up slave families and sold the children to other plantations. Slaves often lived in broken-down cabins. They lacked basic necessities, such as enough food and clothing.

The Civil War

By the middle of the 1800s, Americans were involved in a heated argument about whether the practice of slavery should expand in the United States. Many people in the South wanted slavery to continue and grow. Their economy depended on it. They realized their region could not prosper as it had without the free labor of slaves. Many people in the North, on the other hand, wanted to ban the import, sale, and use of slaves. This argument over slavery and another fight over states' rights caused the Civil War, which began in 1861. That is when southern states began to secede, or withdraw, from the Union. South Carolina was the first to do so.

On February 18, 1861, Jefferson Davis, a distinguished former United States Army officer and senator from Mississippi, was inaugurated as President of the Confederate States of America. When the southern states surrendered, the United States government imprisoned Davis for two years and stripped him of his United States citizenship for betraying the Union. He was later freed.

Mississippi became the second state to secede, on January 9, 1861. The southern states then formed their own new nation, which they called the Confederate States of America.

The Civil War was a devastating period for Mississippi. The Union and Confederate armies fought many important battles in the state. A ferocious battle took place at Vicksburg when Union soldiers occupied the city during a forty-seven-day siege. The Union soldiers took over the port and destroyed businesses, churches, and homes. Confederate soldiers fought hard to defend Vicksburg during the siege. But without incoming food, supplies, and reinforcements, Confederate soldiers in Vicksburg finally surrendered.

Some Vicksburg residents hid in forests and caves outside their city in order to escape the deadly fighting in 1863.

Of the 78,000 Mississippi men and boys who fought for the Confederate army, approximately 12,000 died in battle, and 15,000 died of disease. When the rest finally made it home, many men were wounded and sick. They had been weakened by their lack of food, warm clothing, and shoes. The women, children, and old people who remained at home after their men folk joined the war effort also suffered terribly. Many women bravely took on the kind of hard, physical work formerly done by their men. And, like the soldiers, the women endured hunger, poverty, and sickness.

Mississippi's black population suffered during the Civil War as well. However, their future seemed brighter when President Abraham Lincoln declared all slaves to be free. While Lincoln's Emancipation Proclamation did free all slaves, life was still hard. There were few jobs to be had during or after the war for people of any color. Like many white families, black families found it difficult to feed, house, and clothe themselves.

After the Civil War

Hard times continued in Mississippi during the years after the Civil War. The United States government declared that the southern states could reenter the Union, but first these states had to undergo reconstruction. The United States government used its army to run the southern states. It placed all of them, including Mississippi, under military law. The federal government told the southern states when elections would be held and dictated who could run for office.

During this Reconstruction Era, Mississippi drew up a new state constitution. The constitution allowed blacks the right to vote and to hold political office. It also made all children eligible for free public education. Although black Mississippians enjoyed newfound freedoms for a time, those liberties did not last. After Mississippi was formally readmitted to the Union, white politicians worked to regain the political power they had lost. They passed a new constitution that denied the state's black population many basic rights, such as the right to vote and the right to own property.

Change Comes Slowly

Mississippi's economy remained devastated for many decades after the Civil War. Without slave labor, the state never became rich again from cotton. After many big plantations fell into ruin, small farmers struggled to grow crops they could sell for a decent profit. These small farmers, called sharecroppers, leased land from large landowners to whom they had to pay part of every crop. But this tenant farm system made it hard for sharecroppers to get ahead financially. For decades, Mississippi remained one of the poorest states in the United States.

More hard times were on the way. In the 1920s, a devastating flood caused a hundred thousand Mississippians to leave their homes. When the country entered the Great Depression in 1929, Mississippians suffered some more.

Both black and white sharecroppers throughout the South struggled to make a living on farms.

Many of them found it so hard to earn a living that they fled Mississippi. They headed north, hoping to find work in factories in cities such as New York, Philadelphia, and Chicago. But times were tough across the country, with businesses closing and many people without jobs. The government established programs to help the unemployed. The economy also improved when the country entered World War II. Jobs were created as supplies were needed for the war effort.

During this time, many blacks left Mississippi to escape racism. State laws kept segregation in place in Mississippi until well into the 1960s. Segregation laws stated, for example, that black people could not use the same facilities as whites. African Americans could not eat in certain restaurants or attend the same schools. In addition, African Americans continued to be denied the right to vote.

Beginning in the late 1950s, brave individuals began to fight this unfair system and the Civil Rights Movement got under way. In the 1960s, things got ugly in Mississippi between people who wanted to work for racial equality and those who wanted to keep segregation laws. Race riots broke out after a young man named James Meredith tried to become the first black student to enroll at the University of Mississippi. When President John F. Kennedy sent federal troops to try to stop the riots, the troops came under attack.

In 1963, Medgar Evers, a civil rights leader, was killed outside his home in Jackson. It took three trials, and nearly three decades until the suspect, Byron de la Beckwith, was convicted of the murder in 1994.

In 1965, the passage of the Voting Rights Act by Congress meant that Mississippi state officials could no longer deny

African Americans the chance to vote. From that point on, Mississippi's black population steadily gained political power. The situation improved, although racism and poverty was a problem for the state for many more years.

The 1966 March Against Fear at the Mississippi State Capital marked a turning point in the struggle for civil rights for all people.

In 1969, the Supreme Court ruled in favor of desegregation. That meant both black and white children had to attend the same schools. Desegregation did not go well at first. Many white parents removed their children from public schools and sent them to private schools instead. At the same time, the number of black school principals and teachers actually declined, as parents pressured schools to hire whites only. However, many educational reforms took place in the 1980s, and the quality of public education in Mississippi improved.

Mississippi's economy also grew in the 1980s and the 1990s. Agriculture became more varied and no longer depended so heavily on cotton. The state also began to promote tourism and invited visitors to enjoy its wild natural areas and historic sites. Tourism created many new jobs in hotels, restaurants, parks, historic sites, and riverboat casinos.

Important Dates

1540 Spaniard Hernando De Soto leads the first group of Europeans across what is present-day Mississippi on a search for treasure through the South.

1673 French explorers Jacques Marquette and Louis Jolliet begin exploration of the Mississippi River.

1682 René-Robert Cavelier Sieur de LaSalle travels the Mississippi River, claiming all lands drained by the river for the king of France.

1699 The French build Fort Maurepas, the first French settlement in what will become Mississippi, near Biloxi.

LaSalle

1763 The area that is present-day Mississippi passes into English control at the end of the French and Indian War.

1798 The western part of land that will become the state of Mississippi is organized as an American territory.

1803 The Louisiana Purchase opens the Mississippi River to American trade.

1812 The War of 1812 begins.

1817 An Act of Congress admits Mississippi to the Union.

1861 On January 9, Mississippi becomes the second southern state to secede from the Union. The Civil War begins.

1865 The Civil War ends.

1939 Oil is discovered near Tinsley, in Yazoo County.

1964 Congress passes the Civil Rights Act, outlawing segregation in public places. Fannie Lou Hamer helps to organize Freedom Summer, an effort to register African-American voters in Mississippi.

Fanny Lou Hamer

1986 The Tennessee-Tombigbee Waterway is completed.

2005 Hurricane Katrina comes ashore, affecting the states of Mississippi, Louisiana, Alabama, Florida, and parts of Texas. It causes billions of dollars in damage and kills more than a thousand people.

3 The People

Five hundred years ago, only Native Americans lived in the region that would later become Mississippi. Even after European explorers reported that the land had the possibility of becoming a bountiful place to live, few white settlers came. When some French settlers arrived in 1699, they settled near present-day Biloxi. The area seemed to offer a natural port for shipping, rich soil for farming, and fresh drinking water in its rivers.

By the early 1700s, Native Americans shared the land with just a few French neighbors. The second French settlement in the area was founded only in 1716. However, one new development changed everything—the arrival of slaves whom the French had brought to the area from Africa. Slaves who could work the land without pay changed the area's fortunes and population. With free labor, the land could be farmed for great profit. This possibility attracted the interest of Great Britain, Spain, and France. Great Britain already had settlers in the northeast and Spain had settlers in the southwest. Soon Great Britain and France were fighting over land claims.

Children enjoy a fair in Natchez.

France finally gave up its land claims to Great Britain after they lost the French and Indian War in 1760.

During the short period between that war and the outbreak of the American Revolution, most of the settlers who arrived in the area were British. They came from England, Ireland, Scotland, and Wales. Spain also sent settlers to America. During the Revolution, Spain took the opportunity to seize control of West Florida, which contained part of present-day Mississippi.

After the United States gained its independence from Great Britain in 1783, the population grew quickly. Native Americans, white settlers from Europe, and slaves from Africa made up the population. Newcomers kept arriving in great numbers.

By 1800, about seven thousand Native Americans still lived in what is now Mississippi. In the Natchez area alone, the population numbered between 4,000 and 5,000 whites and blacks, which made it quite a sizeable city for its time. Approximately 1,200 white settlers and slaves lived along the Tombigbee River.

Increasing numbers of white settlers pushed Native Americans from the territories where their people had lived for thousands of years. In 1816, one traveler reported that 4,000 settlers came to the Mississippi River area in just nine days. Between 1810 and 1820, the population soared from approximately 37,000 people to about 75,000 people (both of these counts included slaves). By 1860, the population had grown tenfold to more than nearly 800,000 people. On the eve of the American Civil War, Mississippi's population was about evenly divided between black and white people.

A Choctaw boy dances at a festival on the reservation in Philadelphia, Mississippi.

Growth slowed significantly after the end of slavery weakened the economy. New settlers found other parts of the United States more attractive than the southern United States. By 1900, Mississippi had just over 1.5 million people. Between 1910 and 1920, the population actually decreased by several thousand. Mississippi's population went through a series of small increases followed by small decreases over the next few decades.

African Americans made up the majority of Mississippi's population until 1940. Today, however, 61 percent of Mississippi's population is white. African Americans make up approximately 37 percent of Mississippians. The state has the highest percentage of black people of any state.

In 2005, around 921,088 people lived in the state. And while the state's population is growing fast today, it has remained relatively small compared with other states. Mississippi's entire population is smaller than the city of Chicago.

In 2005, around 20,400 Asians and Asian Americans lived in Mississippi. This included two new groups of Asian immigrants. Filipinos (people from the Philippines) and Vietnamese people moved to the state. Many came to work in Mississippi's fishing and shrimping industries, while others worked in other Mississippi industries.

The number of Hispanics is increasing rapidly in Mississippi. In 1990, fewer than 16,000 Mexican Americans lived in the state. In 2004 there were more than 49,000 Hispanic residents. The Hispanic population continues to increase. Many of them are Mexican Americans or Mexicans who have come to the state to

The first Spaniards who passed through what is now Mississippi came and left the area quickly. Today's Hispanic families are among the fastest-growing groups of residents in the state.

work in agriculture. Hispanic populations are growing in Mississippi's cities as well.

In a state with so many agricultural resources, most Mississippians have long chosen to live in rural farming areas. Mississippi's cities are small. Its largest city, Jackson, has a population of approximately 200,000 people. Biloxi, the next biggest city, is just a quarter the size of Jackson. Greenville, Hattiesburg, Meridian, and Gulfport also have populations of more than 40,000. Fewer than 400,000 of the state's residents live in a sizeable city.

Small town storefronts in some parts of Mississippi look much the way they did a hundred years ago.

Ethnic Influences Today

Today, as in the past, people of diverse origins call Mississippi home. Many of the state's residents have lived in the state all their lives, but Mississippi's population also includes many people who have only recently arrived. Some of these are immigrants, people who have come from another country to live and to work in the United States. Others have moved to Mississippi from elsewhere in the United States. Some families come because of job opportunities. But many people who move to Mississippi are retirees. They come to spend their later years enjoying the state's restful environment, mild climate, and beautiful scenery.

A variety of ethnic influences can be seen in the state of Mississippi. Native American culture is still visible. Tourists visit the state to see evidence of the great Mound Builder civilization that developed here a thousand years ago. Although the Mound Builders are long gone, their descendents in other Native American groups remain in Mississippi.

Some descendants of the Chickasaw, the Choctaw, and the Natchez who were living there when the French arrived in the seventeenth century continue to live in Mississippi. The current Natchez Native American population is small and scattered throughout the state, as is the Chickasaw. Nevertheless, museums and cultural centers celebrate their heritage. Mississippi has always had a larger number of Choctaw. Today thousands live on the Choctaw Reservation, located on Highway 16, in the middle of the state near the town of Philadelphia.

Despite the early Spanish explorations, little of that early Spanish influence remains visible today. The French, who followed the Spaniards into the area, left their mark in a few place names, such as Bienville and Bay St. Louis. Louisville was named after France's King Louis XIV. As recently as one hundred years ago, though, so many people of French descent still lived in the state that French classes were taught in most Mississippi schools. According to one historian, "many people born in the early twentieth century can recall relatives who spoke only or mainly French."

One can also see a few signs of Asian influence in Mississippi. The Chinese, who came to work on cotton plantations in the nineteenth century after the slaves were freed, formed a tightly knit group. One group from China's Sze Yap district, first lived in Washington County. Later on, another group owned land in Boliver County. A few Chinese grocery stores can be found around Mississippi.

Many Vietnamese have settled in Mississippi to work in the shrimp industry. A large number of them lost their shrimp boats and shrimp factory jobs after Hurricane Katrina hit the Gulf Coast.

The town of Greenville has a separate Chinese cemetery. Today you can also see store signs written in Vietnamese in Biloxi and other places along the coast where Vietnamese work as shrimpers. One of the most significant changes in Mississippi's population in recent years has been in the number of Asian Americans living there.

The larger number of African Americans, on the other hand, have had a big influence on life in Mississippi. Many of them own farms and businesses. Some are active in politics. Particularly in the Delta Region, African-American musicians have created a unique kind of music called the blues. Some of this music has a haunting, mournful sound, while some blues are lively and fast. Once a branch of folk music, the blues have greatly influenced music, especially rock and roll.

Musicians of many races and musical styles have embraced the blues that African Americans developed in the Mississippi Delta.

Mississippi for Visitors

Mississippians cherish their heritage. They have preserved many of the state's elegant old homes and neighborhoods. Historical sites also include reminders of difficult times in Mississippi's history, particularly its years of slavery and the Civil War. A historical marker at the site of Natchez's Forks of the Road notes the location of a slave market. Civil War buffs can visit many of Mississippi's battle sites, some of which have been turned into parks or posted with historical markers. Some Civil War groups stage reenactments of famous battles.

Many Mississippians also enjoy sports and the outdoors. Along with out-of-state tourists, they flock to the state's parks, waterways, and other natural areas. Many Mississippians like to hunt, fish, and hike. The state boasts forty-one state wildlife management areas, twelve national wildlife refuges, and six national forests.

Reminders of the Civil War are never far away in Mississippi.

Visitors to the Panther Swamp National Wildlife Refuge, for example, can observe American alligators, otters, swamp rabbits, and mink living in the wild. Visitors to the Gulf Islands National Seashore can sunbathe, swim, or enjoy boating along the white beaches and sparkling ocean. Coastal marshes are popular places for hikers. Mississippi's many rivers, lakes, bayous, and oceans are paradises for the state's fishermen and women.

Birdwatchers spot plenty of birds near Mississippi's many waterways.

Many residents of Mississippi are avid sports fans. Residents closely follow state universities' teams, including the University of Mississippi Rebels and Mississippi State's Bulldogs.

Eating in this top agricultural and fishing state is a delicious experience for Mississippians and tourists alike. Mississippi catfish farmers grow 80 percent of all the catfish eaten in the United States. Fried catfish is a favorite dish throughout the state. Mississippi is famous for its dark rich soil—and for its Mississippi mud pies. This thick, gooey chocolate pie resembles the state's thick, dark mud seen in swamps, riverbanks, and bottomlands. Visitors can find sweet potato dishes on restaurant menus throughout the state, a major sweet potato grower. Sweet potato pie is a special favorite at Thanksgiving around the country, but especially in Mississippi. The Mississippi shrimp boils are a delicious feature of many outdoor festivals as well as firehouse and church suppers. Shrimp boils are big pots of shrimp along with meats, vegetables, and spices.

Art and music lovers can find museums, galleries, and concert halls all over the state. Its fine art museums include the Ohr-O'Keefe Museum of Art in Biloxi, the Walter Anderson Museum of Art in Ocean Springs, the Lauren Rogers Museum of Art in Laurel, and the Mississippi Museum of Art in Jackson.

Classical music lovers attend concerts in Jackson, which has its own symphony, and at colleges and universities around the state. Mississippians listen to great music, not just in concert halls, but in churches, at country fairs, and family reunions.

The Delta Region has been home to more than one hundred great blues musicians, including Howlin' Wolf, Muddy Waters, and B.B. King. These singers greatly influenced the Beatles, Rolling Stones, and other rock and roll singers.

Mississippi's many festivals attract families from all over to celebrate the state's rich land, its history, talented people, great food, wonderful music, and colorful art. The town of Tupelo celebrates the birth of the King of Rock and Roll there by throwing an Elvis Presley Festival once a year. It is also fun to go to Vicksburg's Riverfest, as well as other events.

Devastated areas of Mississippi that are being rebuilt after Hurricane Katrina, include festival locations, parks, and historic and cultural sites. These plans are signs of Mississippians' pride in their state and high hopes for its future.

A modern smokestack and a Civil War courthouse are both part of today's landscape in the bustling port city of Vicksburg.

Famous Mississippians

Jefferson Davis: Confederate President

Jefferson Davis was four years old in 1812 when his family moved from Kentucky to what was then the Mississippi Territory. Davis grew up in a wilderness area, later went off to college in Kentucky, then graduated from West Point, the Army military academy, in 1828. A decorated soldier who fought for the United States in the Mexican War, Davis went on to become an influential United States senator. When the Civil War broke out, he led the Southern cause as its president. At the end of the war, Davis was imprisoned for fighting against the United States. After his release, he returned to his beautiful home in Mississippi.

William Faulkner: Author

Winner of the 1949 Nobel Prize in Literature, William Faulkner was not only born and raised in Mississippi, he also used the state as the setting in many of his books. He grew up in Oxford, but in his novels, Faulkner renamed the town Jefferson. Faulkner died in 1962.

Jim Henson: Muppet Creator

Jim Henson was born in 1936 in Greenville, Mississippi, but was raised in Leland. He created the "Sesame Street" Muppets, including Kermit, Miss Piggy, Big Bird, Cookie Monster, Bert and Ernie, and Gonzo. Henson died in 1990. The town of Leland has opened a Jim Henson Museum honoring his work.

B. B. King: Blues Musician

B. B. King, one of the world's great blues musicians, was born in Itta Bena in 1925. He was the child of a sharecropper, and as a little boy went out into the fields to pick cotton. He first played the guitar as a child. By the 1940s, he was performing on the radio. In the 1950s, he had a long string of hit songs. Today a new generation loves to listen to him play his guitar, which he has named Lucille.

Elvis Presley:
Rock and Roll Musician

Elvis Presley, called the King of Rock and Roll, was born in Tupelo in 1935. One of the greatest musicians of all time, Elvis had 149 songs on Billboard Magazine's "Hot 100 Pop Chart." Eighteen of them occupied the top spot on the charts. That achievement has never been matched by another singer. Visitors still flock to Tupelo to see the tiny house that was his birthplace. Elvis died in 1977.

Leontyne Price: Opera Singer

Mississippi has been the birthplace of many great musicians. Not all of them, however, have played the blues or rock and roll. Leontyne Price became one of the first African-American opera superstars. Born in 1927, Price was raised in a segregated neighborhood in Laurel, Mississippi. A local family she sang for helped the young singer to go to the nation's top music school. She became famous after her performance in 1954 in the folk opera, Porgy and Bess. *She went on to sing leading roles in classical operas, such as* Aida, Tosca, *and* Antony and Cleopatra.

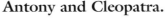

Calendar of Events

Dixie National Rodeo and Livestock Show

The city of Jackson hosts this celebration every January through early February. The event includes a parade, a rodeo, several livestock shows (including one where kids show off the farm animals they have raised), a dance, and more.

Mardi Gras

These celebrations are held on the Gulf Coast and in Natchez every year at the beginning of Lent, which falls in February or March. People celebrate Mardi Gras by dressing up in outrageous costumes and going to carnivals and parades.

Annual World Catfish Festival

Mississippi's catfish are honored each year in April in Belzoni. The town hosts a fishing competition and a catfish-eating contest.

Mississippi Mule Festival

Every May, the town of Bay Springs honors the state's hard-working farm mules. Events include storytelling, a race in which mules pull heavy loads, the Gold Rush during which children try to find money in haystacks, and a southern dance called a cake walk.

Choctaw Indian Fair

The Choctaw community invites everyone to come to its fair, held every July, on their reservation in Philadelphia, Mississippi. Visitors flock to the event to see these Native Americans dancing, playing music, wearing traditional dress, and displaying their arts and crafts.

Roscoe Turner Balloon Races

Roscoe Turner Hot Air Balloon Races

Every August, the skies over Corinth fill with colorful hot air balloons. This event celebrates the life of Roscoe Turner, a hometown boy who became famous as a barnstormer, or trick pilot.

Mississippi Delta Blues and Heritage Festival

In Greenville, music is in the air every September thanks to its many concerts. Musicians celebrate Mississippi's Delta blues tradition with nonstop music during the festival.

Blessing of the Shrimp Fleet and Seafood Festival

A special ceremony every May honors fishermen and shrimp harvesters who died at sea. A wreath is dropped into the water at the Biloxi Yacht Club pier. A bishop blesses the boats as they participate in a procession. The Biloxi Seafood Festival in September is another seaside celebration. Events include a schooner boat race and shrimp eating feasts.

Mississippi State Fair

In this rich farming state, the fall harvest is celebrated in Jackson every October. One of the South's largest state fairs, the fair gives farmers a chance to show off their finest stock animals and produce. There are also carnival rides and plenty to eat.

Sweet Potato Festival

Vardaman, which calls itself the Sweet Potato Capital of the World, honors its favorite crop every November. Visitors sample all kinds of sweet potatoes.

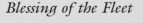

Blessing of the Fleet

4 How It Works

Mississippi, like other states, has several levels of government that serve its people at different levels—federal, state, county, city, or town.

Citizens of every state, including Mississippi, elect two United States senators every six years. The number of representatives a state has in the United States House of Representatives varies according to the size of its population. Mississippi has six representatives—Congressman or Congresswoman—who are elected every two years. Both senators and representatives work on behalf of all Americans. But they also pay special attention to the needs and concerns of the people of their own state. Mississippians also participate in the United States presidential elections, which are held every four years.

The Federal Building in Jackson is named after Dr. A.H. McCoy, a prominent business leader. It was the first federal building in the nation named in honor of an African American.

The Mississippi State Capitol in Jackson.

The Political History of Mississippi

Mississippi became a state in 1817. When it formally entered the Union as a state, Mississippi needed a state constitution. Political leaders wrote one immediately. Three other versions followed, in 1832, 1869, and 1890.

The state constitution spells out how the state's government works. Mississippi's constitution, in its current form, provides for a governor and lieutenant governor to be elected every four years. These officials can serve only two terms in a row. However, there is no limit to the number of terms they can serve in total. The constitution also spells out which other officers are to be elected, rather than appointed. As in other states, Mississippi also has a two-chamber legislature and a court system.

The Mississippi Band of Choctaw Indians has its own government. Recognized by the United States government since 1945, the Choctaw people have their own constitution. It spells out the organization of a Choctaw government council that represents all its members.

Like other voters in the United States, many Mississippians belong to one of the two major political parties: the Democrats or the Republicans. As in most of the country, the majority of Mississippi's local, state, and national representatives belong to one of those two political groups.

For most of the state's history, the Democratic Party dominated Mississippi's politics. Some Republicans were voted into some offices during the Reconstruction Era, when many former Confederate soldiers were denied the right to vote. But every governor of the state between 1876 and 1991 was a Democrat. That changed in 1991 when Kirk Fordice became the first Republican elected to the state's highest office in more than one hundred years.

Marchers protesting the murders of three civil rights workers in 1964 demonstrated their outrage in a procession to Philadelphia, Mississippi.

The right to vote was restricted for most of Mississippi's history. Women did not win voting rights until the 1920s. In a new state constitution in 1890, Mississippi curbed African Americans' right to vote, though they had been able to vote during the Reconstruction Era. In protests and marches, African Americans, along with many whites, pressured the federal government to pass the Voting Rights Act of 1964. This law gave African Americans the right to vote again in their states.

How a Bill Becomes a State Law

The power to make and pass laws in Mississippi involves the governor as well as state legislators elected to one of two "houses." These houses are the state senate and the house of representatives. A senator or a house representative may introduce a bill (a proposed law) of interest to citizens. The senator or representative reads the bill in his or her house.

Branches of Government

The state government in Mississippi is divided into three branches, as in other states.

Executive The executive branch is charged with preparing budgets and making sure the laws passed by the legislative branch are carried out. This branch includes the governor, lieutenant governor, and other officials such as the secretary of state, treasurer, auditor, and the attorney general.

Legislative The legislative branch is made up of the state senate, with 52 members, and the house of representatives, which has 122 members. Its job is to make and pass state laws.

Judicial At the top of the judicial branch sits the Mississippi supreme court, court of appeals, and trial courts. Lower courts include circuit courts, chancery courts, county courts, justice courts, and municipal or town courts. All the courts rule on matters of state law.

Leaders of that house assign the bill to a committee that specializes in the issue. This might be education, transportation, or the environment, for example. The special committee studies the bill. When it decides the entire senate or house should hear the bill, the committee schedules a date to do so. After the bill is read, it is put to a vote. If the bill passes in the house where it was read, it is sent to the other house, where the bill goes through the same process.

Bills may be sent back and forth depending on changes that representatives make along the way. Sometimes a bill goes straight to the governor, who signs it into law. However, sometimes the governor vetoes, or refuses to sign the bill. When that happens, the bill may go back to the senate or house of representatives for more changes. The governor may then sign it. However, if the governor still vetoes the bill, the legislators can still get it passed. They can override the governor's veto if they have enough votes to pass the bill.

A bill may also go back to the legislature for changes before it ever gets to the governor. At each step, the legislators, including the special committees, must review the changes in the bill before it goes to the governor. The result is called a compromise bill (one that must satisfy both houses).

How the State's Local Government Works

Mississippi is divided into eighty-two counties. Unlike the systems in many other states, an elected five-member board of supervisors runs each county. County boards of supervisors set property taxes. They may decide such matters as which county roads big trucks may travel on, for example. The state also has a total of more than 290 cities and towns with their own local governments. The mayors of most of these cities and towns work with an elected council to make decisions concerning local laws and their enforcement. Mayors and councils pass laws that affect the people who live in their town. They might decide, for instance, where new factories can be built. (Such matters are covered by what are called zoning laws.)

In 1969, the state elected its first black mayor since Reconstruction. Charles Evers, brother of civil rights leader Medgar Evers, was elected in the city of Fayette.

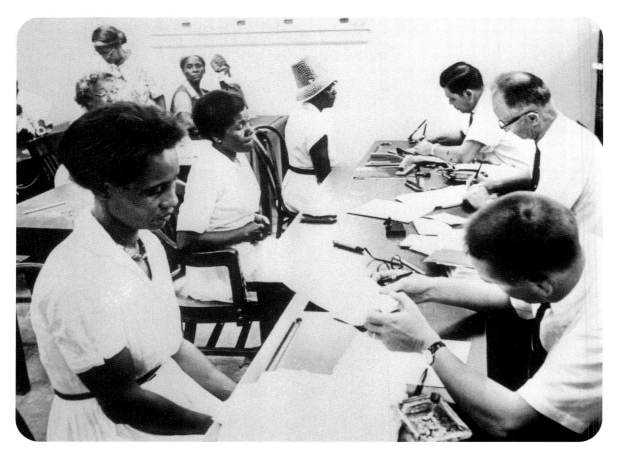

In the 1960s, the federal government sent representatives to help unregistered Mississippi residents to vote for the first time.

Hot Topics

Just as in other states, political issues come and go in Mississippi. In 2005, residents of the state were concerned about how much help the federal government would be able to provide to rebuild after Katrina. At the state level, the governor and legislature were especially concerned about funding Mississippi's schools.

Mississippians participate in their government and voice their opinions. They write, e-mail, and call their legislators to talk about the issues that concern them. Legislation is often shaped by the voice of the people. By learning about issues, everyone can make a difference.

In 1993, the state's National Association for the Advancement of Colored People, filed a lawsuit in a county court against the governor, attempting to force him to change the flag. Instead, a commission studied the matter and came up with a new design. In 2001, the commission asked citizens to vote on whether to adopt it or keep the old flag. When the votes were counted, nearly two-thirds had been cast in favor of keeping the 1894 flag.

This kind of public activism keeps Mississippians involved in their government. As in the case of the state flag, citizens decided to keep a reminder of their past. In other issues, Mississippians will decide the future by their votes and by reminding the people they elect to listen to their voices.

To find Mississippi's state legislators, go to this Web site
www.mississippi.gov
and click on "Mississippi Government" then click "Locate Members of the House of Representatives" or "Locate State Senators." To find Mississippi's representatives to the United States Congress, go to senate.gov and click on "Mississippi." You can ask a parent, teacher, or librarian to help you find out what district you live in.

5 Making a Living

For hundreds of years, most of Mississippi's wealth came from cotton growing. In fact, cotton made Mississippi one of the richest states in the Union 150 years ago. But today, profits from cotton growing make up a much smaller share of Mississippi's income.

In the years between the end of the Civil War and the beginning of World War II, many people in the state struggled to support themselves, as there were too few high-paying jobs. Today, however, the situation has changed. The state government and private citizens have made successful efforts to attract new industries to Mississippi.

As in other parts of the United States, most people find employment in the service sector. That means they might work in banks or business offices, for example. Professional service jobs include those held by doctors, nurses, and lawyers. Tens of thousands of other people in the state hold some kind of government job, working for the federal, state, or local government. These people teach, govern, or work in state agencies—some as

> Dr. James Hardy performed the world's first heart transplant at the University of Mississippi's Medical Center in 1964.

Farmers have been growing cotton in Mississippi's rich soil for centuries.

social workers, administrators, and managers, for example. Tourism is a major industry that creates many other kinds of service jobs in hotels, restaurants, casinos, and major tourists sites. Other workers manufacture goods in Mississippi's factories.

Agriculture

The rich land of Mississippi has provided waves of newcomers with a way to feed their populations and grow cash crops. In some periods, such as the time before the Civil War, Mississippi supported vast farmlands that made some people wealthy. Then war, social changes such as the end of slavery, and agricultural competition altered Mississippi's farm economy. Some Mississippians who grew food and cash crops hit difficult times.

In 1929, the Great Depression began. During this period, the national economy collapsed. Mississippi still remained a farming state, but a poor one. In 1936, the state government began to make an effort to change the nature of the state's economy. It created a new program called Balance Agriculture with Industry. In the years that followed, more and more factories opened across the state. These included furniture and clothing manufacturers that could take advantage of Mississippi's lumber and cotton.

Today the people of Mississippi make their living in a variety of ways. Still, agriculture remains the state's most important economic base. Mississippi continues to produce

Although Mississippi has created new jobs, many of them are low paying. Mississippi is one of the states with the largest percentage of people living in poverty.

more than two million bales of cotton every year. That is close to one fifth of all the cotton that the United States' textile mills make into cloth every year. Cotton seeds are also crushed to make oil and shortening that are used in food processing. Cottonseed feed is also used for livestock.

Although cotton remains a major crop, farmers also grow different kinds of crops. Beginning around the 1930s, they began to produce large amounts of soybeans, for example, and crops used for livestock feed. Today, Mississippi has become known for its sweet potatoes, as well as for its pecans, which grow in the state's many orchards.

Other major crops include rice, hay, wheat, and corn. Livestock and livestock products provide about 54 percent of Mississippi's yearly farm income. Chickens and beef cattle are the state's most valuable livestock. Mississippi usually ranks among the top five states in marketing broilers (chickens), and farmers also sell large numbers of hogs and chicken eggs as well as substantial amounts of dairy products.

Farmland once devoted to growing cotton now supports other crops like livestock feed for Mississippi's cattle.

Recipe for Sweet and Spicy Pecans

Pecan trees grew in the wild long before people came to the southern part of what became North America. These nutritious nuts were an important part of the diets of Native American and European settlers. Later, settlers began to cultivate, or grow, pecan trees as a cash crop. Today, Mississippi growers produce over 6 million pounds of pecans a year. The nuts are a delicious ingredient in pies, vegetable and meat dishes, candies, and snacks.

Ingredients:

2 cups pecan halves

2 tablespoons melted butter in a bowl

1/2 teaspoon of Tabasco hot sauce

1 tablespoon sugar

1/2 teaspoon chili powder

1/2 teaspoon ground cumin

Small pinch of salt

Have an adult help you preheat the oven to 325 degrees Fahrenheit.

Line a baking sheet with foil and set it aside while you prepare the pecans.

Coat the pecans with the melted butter and Tabasco hot sauce. Combine the remaining dry ingredients in a bowl. Pour the dry ingredients over the pecans to coat them.

Spread the pecans on the baking sheet in a single layer. Bake the pecans for 15 minutes, turning the pecans over at least once. (Have an adult help you with this since the baking sheet and the nuts will be hot!)

Remove the baking sheet from oven. Wait for the pecans to cool for about 10 minutes then nibble on this Mississippi treat!

Fishing

Taking advantage of their state's abundant inland waters, many Mississippians make their money from catfish farms. Mississippi leads all states in the production of freshwater catfish on farms, which yield an annual income of more than forty-five million dollars. Mississippians also fish the state's rivers and lakes and harvest shrimp and oysters off the state's southern coast. Pascagoula-Moss Point is one of the nation's leading fishing ports. Biloxi is the state's chief shrimp port.

Inland waterways, as well as Mississippi's Gulf Coast, support a thriving fishing economy in the state.

Lumbering

Thanks to its extensive forests, Mississippi typically ranks among the ten leading states that produce forestry products. Mississippi farmers grow some of the nation's Christmas trees. Forest products also include pine and hardwood lumber as well as pulpwood that is used to make paper. The state's superior lumber has led to the development of factories that make furniture and other wood products. Over two hundred furniture companies in the northeastern corner of Mississippi produce furniture from local lumber cut in the state's sawmills. Since the early 1990s, over a third of the new jobs in the state were in the furniture and wood products industry.

Mississippi's furniture makers and wood carvers stay close to their state's extensive forests to produce their goods.

Manufacturing

Mississippi not only grows cotton, but its textile mills and clothing manufacturers turn that cotton into fabric and clothing right in the state. Other Mississippi factories produce packaged foods, paint, transportation equipment, and electronic equipment. Over 6,000 people work in Mississippi's chemical industry. Some of the chemicals are made from state's oil and mineral resources.

Nearly 70,000 of Mississipi's 243,000 factory jobs were lost after Hurricane Katrina hit Gulf Coast manufacturing areas in 2005. The hurricane damaged so many factories and homes, workers moved away. Pascagoula, a major shipbuilding and transportation equipment center, was hit hard. Mississippi's leaders hope that reconstruction efforts will bring back jobs and workers.

The Navy brought the U.S.S. Cole, which was damaged by a terrorist attack in 2000, to the Ingalls Shipyard in Pascagoula for repairs.

Mississippi has four ports on the Gulf of Mexico: Pascagoula, Biloxi, Gulfport, and Port Bienville. The huge cargo ships that come and go carry millions of tons of products and equipment, including petroleum, ores, lumber, and textiles. A busy Mississippi River port is Vicksburg, which gets the most traffic of all the river ports.

Workers in some of Mississippi's factories produce aerospace equipment and motor vehicle parts. Factories in Tupelo, Columbus, Jackson, and Natchez produce wood products. Corinth and Jackson are the chief centers for producing electronic equipment. Meat packing, poultry processing, the manufacture of cheese, and the canning and freezing of fish are important food industries. Other items manufactured in Mississippi include industrial machinery, chemicals, fabricated metal products, and refined petroleum.

Mississippian, Joseph A. Biedenharn, owner of the Biedenharn Candy Company of Vicksburg, Mississippi, first bottled Coca-Cola. Earlier, the drink was for sale only at the soda fountains in drugstores.

Today the state is a leader in the telecommunications industry, with many long distance telephone and pager companies now operating in Mississippi.

Oil and Gas

In the twentieth century, Mississippians found a new way to make money when oil was discovered for the first time in Yazoo County. The first oil well produced oil in 1939.

Today there are several thousand wells that produce millions of barrels of oil each year. The state also produces a great deal of the country's natural gas.

Other materials mined in Mississippi include sand, gravel, crushed stone, and limestone, as well as clay, marl, cement rock, sandstone, bentonite, and fuller's earth, a kind of clay used in processing certain oils.

New Horizons

For a long time, Mississippi's economy was slow to grow. But in the last twenty years, the state's leaders have worked hard to change that. One way they have done so is to attract tourists and retired people to their state. Each year, several millions of travelers come to Mississippi to enjoy its natural beauty and warm weather. While visiting, they spend money by staying in hotels and motels, buying gas for their cars, eating out at restaurants, and so on. The annual economic benefit of tourism to the state exceeds $1.6 billion.

Many visitors travel along the Natchez Trace Parkway, which follows the route of the Natchez Trace, an important road in the history of Mississippi and the South that connects Natchez and Nashville, Tennessee. Other National Park Service areas in the state are Brices Cross Roads National Battlefield Site (near Tupelo), Gulf Islands National Seashore, Tupelo National Battlefield, and Vicksburg National Military Park. The state maintains a system of twenty-seven parks and recreation areas, including several on major reservoirs.

Products & Resources

Catfish

Mississippi has more catfish farms—around four hundred of them—than any other state. Beginning in the 1960s, many farmers, whose land had been overused for cotton growing, decided to try something new. They began to dig ponds for raising catfish. Today the state exports millions of pounds of the tasty fish every year.

Chickens

In the 1940s, Mississippi farmers started to raise chickens on a large scale. Today thousands of independent contractors raise chickens for huge poultry companies. In one year, Mississippians raise more than seven hundred million birds and earn approximately two billion dollars from the sale of chickens and eggs.

Cotton

In the year 2001, Mississippi farmers planted a record 1.7 million acres in cotton. It is the state's number one agricultural product. Cotton plants yield cotton bolls, which are picked and then pulled apart to make thread that can then be woven into fabric.

Oil and Gas

A long time ago, seas covered all of Mississippi. When the water receded, rich deposits of petroleum and minerals were left behind. In 1939, the news broke that an oil well in Yazoo County had begun to produce. By 1970, the state's wells numbered in the thousands, which together yielded over 65 million barrels of oil every year. Another of the state's natural resources is natural gas, which can be used to generate electricity. Mississippi ranks twelfth in the United States in the production of oil. Today the state has 550 oil and gas fields.

Pine

Pine trees are one of Mississippi's greatest natural resources. They first grew wild in many parts of the state. Today tree farmers also grow pine trees. In fact, the state ranks first in the United States in tree farming. The trees are harvested for lumber, which is used in construction. The state also grows an enormous number of pines for Christmas trees.

Sweet Potatoes

In northern Mississippi, farmers plant about 15,000 acres in sweet potatoes each year. Everyone agrees that sweet potatoes grown in the rich soils of northern Mississippi are especially good. Their sales bring close to $41 million into the state every year.

Looking to the Future

It will be a long time before Mississippi's economy can fully recover from the damage caused by Hurricane Katrina. Almost every Mississippi industry was damaged in some way when the deadly hurricane stormed through the state. The floods that accompanied the hurricane ruined crops and destroyed farms. Industries lost buildings. The service sector suffered because tourist attractions were damaged and closed, so fewer tourists visited the state. Many people lost their jobs when floodwaters and winds damaged their workplaces.

Hurricane Katrina also destroyed houses and schools, so many Mississippians had to move to other places. Some towns lost large portions of their populations due to death or because people left after their homes or businesses were destroyed.

Later, however, the effects of the hurricane also created new jobs in construction to rebuild the cities and towns. Shortly after the floodwaters receded in Biloxi, for instance, architects and other city planners began to create a new vision for what buildings and communities along the coast might look like.

Mississippians have endured many hard times recently and in the past. But its people are rebuilding with determination and strength. They are committed to remaking it an even better state than ever.

The 113-year old Mississippi flag has a square in the corner with thirteen stars. These are said to represent the thirteen original colonies of the United States. It is called the "union square" or "canton corner." However, during the period when the South formed the Confederate States of America, the stars represented the thirteen southern states in the Confederacy. The three equal bars are blue, white, and red—the colors of the United States flag—and represent the Confederate battle flag.

In the center of Mississippi's state seal is an eagle. Across its chest lies a shield, with stars at the top and stripes down below. The eagle, with widespread wings, clasps both an olive branch and arrows in its talons. This symbolizes that the state desires peace but is prepared to fight.

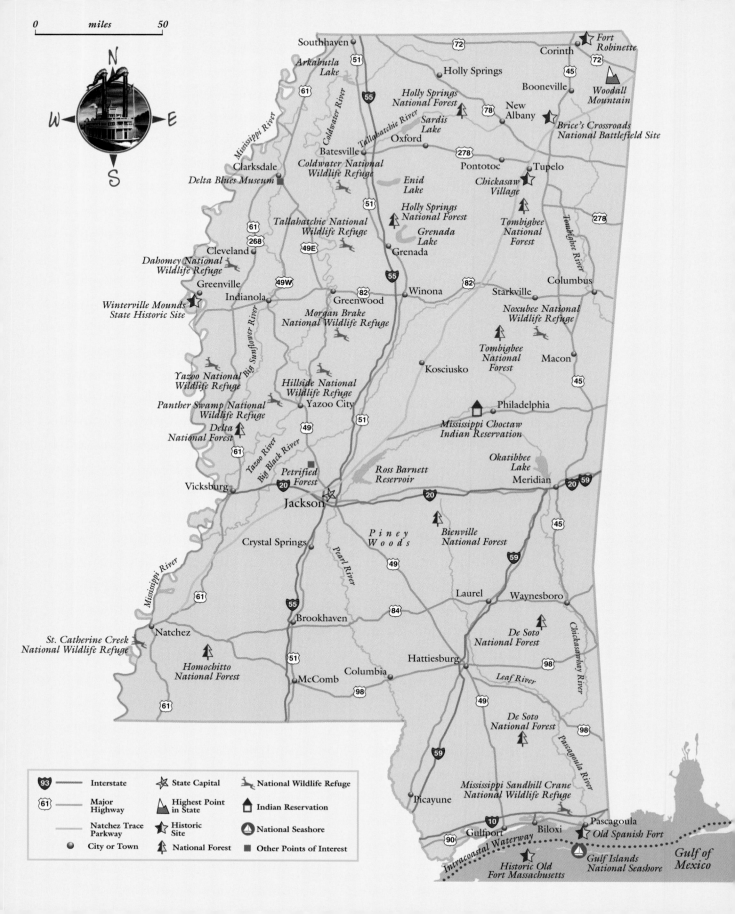

Go, Mississippi!

Words and Music by
William Houston Davis

States may sing their songs of praise, With wav-ing flags and hip-hoo-rays, Let

cym-bals crash and let bells ring 'Cause here's one song I'm proud to sing.

CHORUS

GO, MIS-SIS-SIP-PI, keep roll-ing a-long, ___

GO, MIS-SIS-SIP-PI, you can-not go wrong, ___

GO, MIS-SIS-SIP-PI, we're sing-ing your song, ___

M-I-S — S-I-S — S-I-P-P-I.

State Song

More About Mississippi

Books

Naden, Corinne J. *Mississippi.* Berkeley Heights, NJ: MyReportLinks.com Books, 2003.

Olson, Nathan. *The Mississippi River.* Mankato, MN: Capstone Press, 2004.

Venable, Rose. *The Civil Rights Movement.* Chanhassen, MN: Child's World, 2002.

Web Sites

Mississippi History Now, an online publication of the Mississippi Historical Society,
http://mshistory.k12.ms.us

Mississippi Museum of Natural Science Home Page,
www.mdwfp.com/museum/default.asp

Official State Web Site of Mississippi,
www.mississippi.gov/index.jsp

About the Author

Ann Graham Gaines is a freelance author who lives with her children in a cabin in the woods near Gonzales, Texas.

Index

Page numbers in **boldface** are illustrations.

African Americans, 33, 34, **34**, 35, 36, 37, 41, 46, **46**, 51, 57
  see also slaves
agriculture, 36, 64–65
  see also farming
Alabama, 7, 29, 30
alligators, 17, 19, **19**, 48
animals, 16, 17, 18, **18**, 21, 48
Appalachian Mountains, 8, 13

Bald Cypress, 18, **18**
bayous, 7, 10, 14, 17, 48
Bay St. Louis, 14, 15, **15**, 45
Bienville, 14, 45, 70
Biloxi, 14, 15, 37, 39, 43, 46, 49, 53, 67, 70, 74
birds, 17, **48**
black bear, 19, **19**
British, 28, 29, 39, 40

capital region, 11, 12
catfish, 48, 72, **72**
Chickasaw, 22,23, 26, 44
Chinese, 42,45, 46
Chippewa, 24
Choctaw, 22, 23, 24, 26, 27, 30, **41**, 44, 52, 56
civil rights, 35, **36**, 37, **57**
  see also segregation
Civil War, 31-33, 34, 37, 40, 47, **47**, **49**, 50, 63, 64
Coastal Region, 11, 14, 16, 74
coastline, 9, 14, 16, 17, 22, 48
Confederates, 31, 32, 33, 50, 75
Corinth, 13, 53
cotton, 28, 30, 34, 36, 45, **62**, 63, 64, 65, **65**, **72**

Davis, Jefferson, 31, 50, **50**
de Soto, Hernando, 26, **26**, 27, 37

Delta Region, 11, 46, **46**, 49
  see also Mississippi Delta
d'Iberville, Pierre LeMoyne, 27, **27**

endangered species, 17, **18**, **19**
Europeans, 26, 39, 40, 66
Evers, Charles, 59
Evers, Medgar, 35, 59
explorers, 26, 27, 39

factories, 64, 68, 69
farming, 13, **19**, 21, 22, 23, 30, 34, 39, 43, 46, **62**, 64, 65
Faulkner, William, 50, **50**
festivals, 48, 49, 52, 53
fishing, 17, 21, 42, 47, 48, 67, **67**, **72**
food, 48, 64, 65, 66, 69, 70, **72**, **73**
forests, **13**, 16, 17, **18**, **19**, 21, 23, **32**, 47, 68, **68**, **73**
Fort Maurepas, 27, 28, 37
France, 27, 39, 40, 45
French, 27, 28, 39, 44, 45
French and Indian War, 28, 37, 40

gas, 9, 70, 71, **72**
government, 55-61, 63
Great Depression, **20**, 34, 64
Gulf Intracoastal Waterway, 14, **67**
Gulf of Mexico, 5, 7, 7, 9 10, 14, **27**
Gulfport, 14 15, 43, 70

Hamer, Fannie Lou, 37, **37**
Henson, Jim, 50, **50**
Hills Region, 11, 13
Hispanics, 42, **42**
Hurricane Camille, 14, 15

Hurricane Katrina, 15, **15**, 16, 37, **45**, 49, 60, 69, 74
hurricanes, 14, 15, **15**

Jackson, 12, 35, 43, 49, 52, 53, **54**, 70
Jefferson, Thomas, 29
Jolliet, Louis, 27, 37

King, B.B., 49, 51, **51**
Kennedy, John F., 35

LaSalle, Rene-Robert Cavelier sieur de, 27, 37, **37**
lakes, 10, 11, 14, 17, 48
Lincoln, Abraham, 33
Louis XIV, King, 27, 45
Louisiana, 15, 27, 37
Louisiana Purchase, 29, 37
lumbering, **19**, 64, 70

Madison, James, 29
manufacturing, 69, 70
Mardi Gras, 52,
Marquette, Jacques, 27, 37
Meredith, James, 35
mining, 71
Mississippi Delta, 8, 10, 11, 12, **12**
  see also Delta Region
Mississippi River, 8, **9**, 10, 11, 12, **12**, **18**, 21, 26, 27, 28, 29, 37, 40
Mississippi Sound, 14
Mississippi Territory, 29
Mound Builders, 21, 44
museums, 49, 50
music, 46, 49, 51, 53

Natchez, 23, 30, **30**, 31, **39**, 40 52, 70, 71
Natchez Indians, 24, 26, 27, 44

Natchez Trace Parkway, **13**, 71
Native Americans, **13**, 24, 26, 27, 28, 30, 39, 40, 44, 52, 66
New Orleans, 28, 29

oil, 9, 37, 69, 70, 71, **72**
Oxford, 13, 50
oysters, 17, 19, **19**, 67

Pascagoula, 14, 15, 67, 69, **69**, 70
Pines Region, 11
pitcher plant, 18, **18**
plantations, 28 30 **30**, 31, 34, 45
plants, 16, 17, 18, **18**
population, 12, 39, 40, 41, 42
Presley, Elvis, 13, 49, 51, **51**
Price, Leontyne, 51, **51**

Reconstruction, 33, 56, 57
rivers, 19, 11, 12, 14, 17, 21, 22, 27, 29, 39, 40, 48

Sandhill Crane, 18, **18**
schools, 43, 60
segregation, 35, 37
    see also civil rights
service industry, 63, 64
sharecroppers, 34, **34**, 51
shrimp, 17, 48, 53, 67
slaves, 28, 30, 31, 34, 39, 40, 41, 47, 64
    see also African Americans
Spanish, 26, 27, 28, 29, 39, 40, 44
state
    bird, 4
    borders, 7
    capitol building, **54**
    fish, 5
    flag, 61, 75
    flower, 4
    fossil, 5
    land mammal, 4
    map, 76
    nickname, 4
    seal, 75

song, 77
    water mammal, 5
statehood, 29, 37, 56
sweet potatoes, 48, 53, 73

Tennessee-Tombigee Waterway, **10**, 37
tourism, 36, 44, 47, 64, 71
Tupelo, 13, 16, 49, 70, 71

Vicksburg, 10, 12, 32, **32**, 49, **49**, 70, 71
Vietnamese, 42, **45**, 46
Voting Rights Act, 35, 57

War of 1812, 14, 37
Washington, George, 28
web sites, 61, 76
West Florida, 28, 29, 40